Stanley's
Beauty Contest

For my beautiful daughters, Lia and Tess — L.B.

For my sister Elizabeth, in memory of our childhood dog contests — B.S.

Text © 2009 Linda Bailey
Illustrations © 2009 Bill Slavin

Kids Can Press acknowledges the financial support of the Government of Ontario, through the Ontario Media Development Corporation's Ontario Book Initiative; the Ontario Arts Council; the Canada Council for the Arts; and the Government of Canada, through the BPIDP, for our publishing activity.

Published in Canada by
Kids Can Press Ltd.
29 Birch Avenue
Toronto, ON M4V 1E2

Published in the U.S. by
Kids Can Press Ltd.
2250 Military Road
Tonawanda, NY 14150

www.kidscanpress.com

The artwork in this book was rendered in acrylics, on gessoed paper.
The text is set in Leawood Medium.

Edited by Debbie Rogosin
Designed by Julia Naimska
Printed and bound in China

This book is smyth sewn casebound.

CM 09 0 9 8 7 6 5 4 3 2 1

Library and Archives Canada Cataloguing in Publication

Bailey, Linda, 1948–
Stanley's beauty contest / written by Linda Bailey ; illustrated by Bill Slavin.

ISBN 978-1-55453-318-3

I. Slavin, Bill II. Title.

PS8553.A3644S728 2009   jC813'.54   C2008-903812-6

Kids Can Press is a Corus™ Entertainment company

Stanley's Beauty Contest

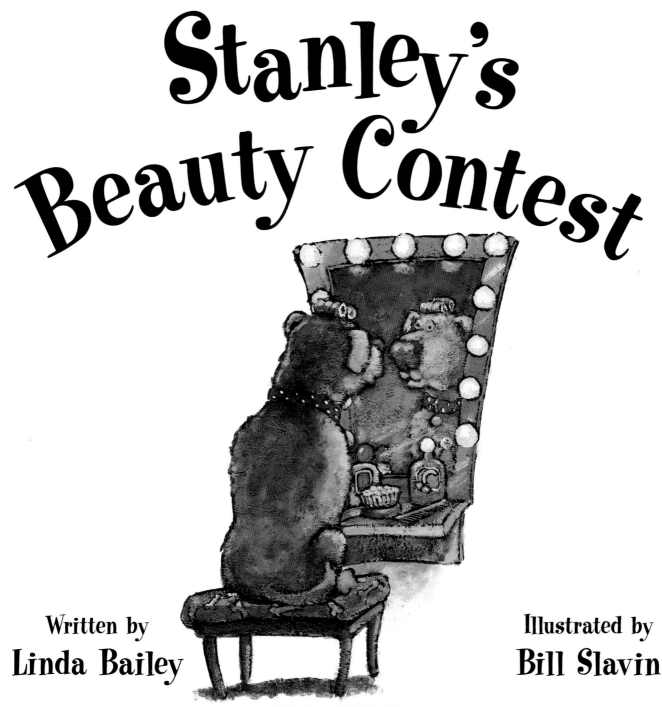

Written by
Linda Bailey

Illustrated by
Bill Slavin

KIDS CAN PRESS

Stanley *knew* he wasn't supposed to jump out of the tub. He was supposed to sit. He was supposed to stay. He was supposed to be a good-dog-Stanley while his people gave him a bath.

But the water was too warm. And he didn't like the gusher thing. And he *hated* the banana shampoo!

So he stood it as long as he could. Then he leaped out and did the only thing a soggy dog can do. He ...

SHOOK!

All over the walls and mirrors. All over the toothbrushes. And especially all over his people.

Then he dove under the bed. His people had to drag him out.

"Arooooo!" howled
Stanley as they blow-dried
his fur.

"Rooooo!" he howled again as
they trimmed his claws and gave
him a sparkly new collar.

But it wasn't till they put him in the car that he really lost his patience.

"Horff, horff, horff!" barked Stanley, trying to run back inside. They'd forgotten his breakfast! They *never* forgot his breakfast!

How could this *happen*, he wondered as he sat fluffy and grumpy and hungry in the back seat.

They drove straight to the park. It was jammed with people and dogs. Some of Stanley's friends were there — Alice and Nutsy and Gassy Jack.

"Hey, Alice," said Stanley in dog talk. "You smell like a raspberry. What's going on?"

"Dog contests," said Alice. "They give a prize to the most beautiful dog."

Nutsy looked puzzled. "How can they tell?"

"Search me," said Alice. "*I* think we all look the same."

"Yup," agreed Gassy Jack. "But we *smell* really weird."

Stanley sniffed his buddies. Gassy Jack smelled like a big sweet pea. Nutsy reeked of peppermint.

"What's wrong with smelling like a *dog*?" asked Gassy Jack.

Suddenly the air filled with a new smell — so rich, so achingly wonderful, every dog in the park stopped to sniff. Bubbling cheese. Sizzling bacon. Hot apple pie. The smells dogs *dream* of in their wildest dreams.

Stanley gasped. "What's that?"

"The prizes," said Alice. "The winners get *those*!"

The dogs stared in wonder as three giant cookies went by, still warm from the oven.

Stanley's stomach tightened. "I could really *use* a cookie," he said. "I didn't get my breakfast."

"That's terrible," said his friends. But they didn't take their eyes off the cookies.

Everyone lined up for the first contest. Fastest Dog.

Hey, thought Stanley, no problem. He could run really *fast* to get one of those cookies. He could run like the wind!

Except he didn't. He tried his best. But he was just getting started when a white blur raced past. A whippet! By the time Stanley reached the finish line, she was already eating the prize.

"Awwrrr," moaned Stanley.

"Never mind," said Alice. "Maybe you'll win Best Tricks."

Stanley perked up. He knew *lots* of tricks. Shake a paw. Roll over. Play dead. He could do them perfectly.

The problem was, the other dogs knew the same tricks. Stanley couldn't believe it. They were doing *his* tricks!

Maybe he could do them faster. Stanley started doing all his tricks at once, really fast. Shake-roll-dead! Shake-roll-dead! Shake-roll-dead! He even threw in some whining.

But there was no prize for whining.

"Awwrrr," moaned Stanley again. It wasn't fair! He was the *hungriest*.

"There's still one prize left," said Alice. "Most Beautiful Dog."

This was it, thought Stanley. His last chance. Somehow, he would have to be ... beautiful! Stanley wasn't exactly sure what beautiful was, but he knew he had to try.

He puffed out his fur. He bared his teeth in a doggy grin. He tried really hard to make his legs straighter and his nose smaller.

But the judges walked right past.

"Rooooo!" howled Stanley as his people took him out of the line. "Roooooooooo!"

He was so disappointed, it took him a whole minute to notice where he was standing. Beside the prize table. And there it was. *Right there!* The very last cookie.

Stanley glanced around. Everyone was watching the beautiful dogs. Nobody was looking at him.

Slowly, he put a paw on the table. Then another.

He wasn't going to *take* the cookie. He was only going to lick it a little. Maybe nibble the edges. Just to make it even.

He rose up high on his tippy-paws, and he reeeeeeeeeeeeeeeeeached ...

Tilt went the table! CRASH went the tray!

Down went the cookie!

Thirty-seven dogs dived on top. It was hard to tell who ate the cookie because in two and a half seconds, it was gone. Stanley *thought* he got a bite, but he wasn't sure.

There was something he *was* sure about, though. For the first time all day ... he was having FUN! *All* the dogs were having fun. What could be more fun than a big pile of dogs?

It was the best dog pile ever!

And it lasted for ages, a great rumble-tumble of rolling and rassling ... till the people said that was *enough* fun! It was time for the dogs to go home.

Nobody was fluffy anymore. Nobody smelled pretty. But every tail was wagging as the dogs left the park!

Stanley's people gave him a scolding in the car. They said he was a bad-dog-Stanley.

But when they saw that they'd forgotten his breakfast, they were very sorry. Stanley knew because they gave him his breakfast *and* his dinner all at once. They scratched behind his ears, too.

As for the other dogs, well, they talked
about that contest for days. They wondered
how it would be if dogs ruled the world and had
contests for the people. Who'd win the prize
for Best-Smelling? Who'd be Most Lick-able?

In the end, they didn't really care. All the dogs loved their own people the best, and after they figured *that* out, all they wanted to do was sniff the breeze and roll in the fresh-mowed grass.

Because that's just how dogs are ...

They may not know everything their people know.

But they sure know what's *important*!